# The boy with the big hair

Written and Illustrated by Khoa Le

INSIGHT KIDS

San Rafael, California

Harry had big bushy hair,
and he never used a comb.
Everybody called him "Hairy."

Whenever his mom tried to brush his hair,
he ran away. "I don't like it," Hairy shouted.

At school, Hairy hid in a
locker when his teacher
tried to comb his hair.

Then, one day, a couple of doves saw Hairy. "Seems like a cozy nest, doesn't it?" the birds said to each other.

So they called Hairy's head their home and started collecting straw to build their nest.

From then on, Hairy had
a pair of tweeting birds
living right on top of his head.

Soon enough, the two birds laid three eggs,
out of which three small chicks hatched.

During music lessons, while all the
boys and girls sang beautifully,
the birds practiced their own song.

The birds sang so loud that the teacher asked Hairy to wait in the hallway all by himself.

One day, Hairy got
caught in the rain.
Soon, a seed in the bird
nest started sprouting.
It quickly grew into a tree.

Very, very quickly.

Soon enough, it was
so big that all kinds of
things got stuck in it.

Then, one day, the little birds were
all grown up and flew away.

. . . only to find new partners . . .

They came back to settle in their parents' nest.
Now Hairy had a whole choir above his head.
The birds were so happy, they sang all day long.

Hairy could no longer stand the noise and ran crying to his mom. His mother took the tree out and placed it in a corner of their garden that was full of sunshine. She then gave Hairy a lovely new haircut.

The garden was even more beautiful thanks to the new tree and all the birds singing their happy songs every day.

KHOA LE is an illustrator, graphic designer, painter, and writer. She graduated from the Fine Arts University in Ho Chi Minh City. She has published thirteen books, seven of which she both wrote and illustrated. Her artwork has been featured in numerous exhibitions in Vietnam, Hong Kong, Singapore, and Korea.

INSIGHT
KIDS

PO Box 3088
San Rafael, CA 94912
www.insighteditions.com

Find us on Facebook: www.facebook.com/InsightEditions
Follow us on Twitter: @insighteditions

First published in the United States in 2016 by Insight Kids,
an imprint of Insight Editions. Originally published in French in Switzerland
in 2014 by NuiNui: © Snake SA 2014.

NuiNui ® is a registered trademark and registered by Snake SA.

nuinui

Translation © Snake SA 2016
Chemin du Tsan Péri 10
3971 Chermignon

Library of Congress Cataloging-in-Publication Data available.

ISBN: 978-1-60887-733-1

ROOTS of PEACE      REPLANTED PAPER

Insight Editions, in association with Roots of Peace, will plant two trees for each tree
used in the manufacturing of this book. Roots of Peace is an internationally renowned
humanitarian organization dedicated to eradicating land mines worldwide and con-
verting war-torn lands into productive farms and wildlife habitats. Roots of Peace
will plant two million fruit and nut trees in Afghanistan and provide farmers there
with the skills and support necessary for sustainable land use.

Manufactured in Shaoguan, China, by Insight Editions

20151201

10 9 8 7 6 5 4 3 2 1